Milton the Mouse

Milton the Mouse

JANICE E. KIRK

RESOURCE *Publications* · Eugene, Oregon

MILTON THE MOUSE

Resource Publications
An Imprint of Wipf and Stock Publishers
199 W. 8th Ave., Suite 3
Eugene, OR 97401

www.wipfandstock.com

PAPERBACK ISBN: 978-1-5326-7203-3
HARDCOVER ISBN: 978-1-5326-7204-0
EBOOK ISBN: 978-1-5326-7205-7

Manufactured in the U.S.A.   01/28/19

Poetry quotations reprinted from *The Poetical Works of John Milton with a Sketch of His Life*, New York: Hurst & Co., 1907.

Chapter 1. "' . . . The stars with deep amaze,/Stand fixed in ste[a]dfast gaze . . . '" *On the Morning of Christ's Nativity, The Hymn VI.*, p. 407, line 27.

Chapter 2. "'. . . Come, let us haste, the stars grow high . . . '" *Comus*, p. 461, line 13.

"'. . . Come and trip it as you go/On the light fantastic toe!'" *L'Allegro*, p. 422, line 5.

Chapter 4. "' . . . But fie my wandering muse/How thou dost stray!'" *Anno Aetatis XIX, (In the Year of his age, 19)* p. 404, line 11.

Chapter 5. "'. . . and sweetly singing round about thy bed, Strew all [his] blessings round bout thy sleeping head?'" *Anno Aetatis XIX*, p. 404, line 21.

Chapter 5. "' . . . and, if it happen as I did forecast,/The daintiest dishes shall be served up last.'"
Anno Aetatis XIX, p. 403, line 11.

Chapter 6. "' . . . thus done the tales, to bed they creep,/By whispering winds soon lulled asleep.'" *L'Allegro*, p. 424, line 7.

Chapter 7. "' . . . Are held with his melodious harmony/In willing chains and sweet captivity,'" *Anno Aetatis XIX*, p. 404, line 9.

Chapter 10. "'. . . And joy shall overtake us as a flood . . . '" *On Time*, p. 414, line 13.

Milton the Mouse Song: "Sport that wrinkled Care derides, And Laughter holding both his sides . . . " *L'Allegro*, p. 422, line 3. " . . . When the merry bells ring round, And the jocund rebecks sound/To many a youth, and many a maid, Dancing in the chequer'd shade . . . " *L'Allegro*, p. 423, line 25.

Dedicated to the memory of my Dad—
A whistle, a poem, a story, a song,
Come fill your pack for the journey.

Contents

Acknowledgments

THIS STORY EVOLVED OVER a span of years, and I thank my friends and family for their faithful readings and feedback on the early versions. In particular I thank my daughter, Amy Guevara, who knew Milton personally and gave me ongoing encouragement. Appreciation goes to Elizabeth Guevara, Jean Hayes, and Margie Obst for their recent careful critiques; as well as Don Kirk and Allan Hansen who joined in the fun. Thanks to Eric Heukeshoven for help with song notation. Special thanks go to editors Caroline Kirk and Maggi Milton, who helped shape this story into its final form. Last but not least I thank Milton, the mouse who hitched a ride home with our family and provided endless fun and delight during the time he lived with us.

1

The Chase

Worn sneakers shuffled closer and closer. Milton dodged into the night shadows.

I wish I had my flashlight," said Kathleen. "Where are those marshmallows?"

Crouched behind the table leg, Milton heard a *rustle*, then a *thump*. "Whoops," said the girl, as something rolled off the camp table and plunked softly in the dirt. Milton leaned forward and sniffed.

Another *rustle*. "Oh, here they are." The sneakers scuffed back to the campfire.

In blink time, Milton bounded forward, mouth watering. He bumped into the soft, white lump that lay in the dirt. He pushed it with his nose. *"Mmm, something delicious."* He pushed it again, and it rolled a little. He sniffed the round sides. *"Where do I bite?"*

"Wow!" cried Matt. "Did you see that?"

Milton dove back under the table, then froze. Beside a pitch–dark boulder that lay in the shadowed grass, two eyes glared at him. PACKRAT!

"A shooting star," yelled the boy by the campfire. "Make a wish!"

"I'm out of here!" wished Milton, as the packrat boldly charged. Milton spun around and crashed into the table leg. Stunned, he staggered up and ran the wrong way, straight for the family.

"I wish for good weather going home." Dad fanned the fire with his old hat.

Milton dodged the hat and the fire ring. He gathered speed as he ran toward the wild roses.

The family gazed upward at the night sky.

"My wish is for coyotes to howl." Kathleen licked her sticky fingers.

"Happy times!" wished Mom, then turned from the fire. "What was that noise?" She peered into the darkness.

The packrat chased Milton along the dark fringe of campfire light. Milton ducked into the grass and bumped against the water–birch tree.

"What's your wish, Matt?" asked Mom.

"Well, I wish I could play the piano better than anyone else!" Matt waved ten fingers in the air and crashed them down on an imaginary piano. "Daaaah, Ta–Dah!" he sang out.

"That's a pretty big wish," said Dad.

Milton scrambled onto a long, narrow branch that curved over the truck tailgate. He flew upwards on the dwindling limb when *"Whoa,"* it sagged with his weight. Too late to stop, he pawed the air and grabbed for leaves and twigs. He swung for a moment over the tailgate, gasping for air. His paws went numb, and with a sickening lurch the last twig slipped away, and everything became a blur. *Whump!* He bounced on cold metal.

Mom gazed upward again. "Look at those stars," she said.

Dazed, Milton opened his eyes. Stars whirled around him with dizzying light.

Dad looked upward at the brilliant Nevada night and intoned, " . . . The stars with deep amaze,/Stand fixed in steadfast gaze . . . .' That's what John Milton, the poet, would say. He's an old friend of mine."

"No way," said Matt. "He wrote that 300 years ago."

"A friend of the heart," Dad placed his hat over his heart and grinned.

"Which ones are the constellations?" asked the girl.

"Squint your eyes, Kathleen," said Matt. "Little stars will disappear. The big groups left over are the constellations."

"Oh," Kathleen squinted, "Matt, where did you learn that?"

"We studied astronomy at school last year," replied Matt. "All the constellations tell a story. It's mythology. There's a bear, a swan, a dragon. Look at those four big stars there, like a cup, and there's the handle. That's the Big Dipper."

"Oh!" said Kathleen. "I see that!"

On the tailgate the mouse lay on his back, breathing heavily. The stars slowed and came to a standstill. *"The stars with deep amaze . . . "* He blinked and rubbed his head, then rolled over and sat up. Behind him the homemade camper sat like a little house on the back of the pickup truck. He peered into the dark doorway, which hid two bunks, cupboards, and a coat closet. He sniffed around the door opening. He loved dark holes, but first he crept along the tailgate to its very edge. It was a long drop to the ground. Milton turned back and ran to the other side, another long drop to the ground. He hunkered down on the cool metal of the tailgate which lay like a flat entry to the camper. He could see the whole camp from here.

The girl crouched by the fire, holding a stick over the coals. She jerked the marshmallow away from the flames. "Perfect. Crusty outside, mushy inside." Gingerly, she pulled the gooey mass off the stick, held it to her lips, and licked. "Ow, it's hot." She blew on it for a moment then popped it into her mouth.

"Where is my other marshmallow?" She reached into her pocket for it, then stopped halfway. She spun toward the picnic table. "What was that?"

"What?" asked Matt.

"I heard something over there," said Kathleen.

Milton listened intently, ready to run.

Matt turned on his flashlight and beamed it toward the table. Something rustled into the bushes.

"Creatures of the night," said Mom.

"*Packrat*," muttered Milton.

"Like what?" Kathleen moved closer to the fire.

"Animals live closer to us than we realize," said Dad. He pulled a small notebook out of his shirt pocket. "A number of nocturnal animals live in this area, and they are all God's creatures."

"Even skunks?" asked Matt.

"Yes, and badgers and bobcats." Dad checked his nature notes.

"*Weasels*," Milton shuddered, "*and that cotton-tailed rabbit in the daytime.*"

"What about packrats and mice," said Mom. "Around that picnic table we drop plenty of crumbs for scavengers."

"They are all on my list. This area is good habitat," said Dad.

"*A nice place to live*," agreed Milton. "*Plenty to eat.*" He looked out at the aspen trees, the wild roses, and the creek. "*Rose hips in the fall. Seeds on the grasses. Water. Pinon nuts, yum.*"

"What do you call this country?" said Matt.

"This is the Great Basin Desert," said Dad. "Know your neighbors. Want to hear about insects, too?"

Matt shook his head. "Not now, Dad. Time for a little music."

"Sure thing," said Dad. He traded his notebook for a harmonica and cradled it in his hands. He leaned forward on his camp chair and blew into the instrument. Notes sang into the night, a silvery-sweet tune that sounded like . . .

Faraway
    moonlit
        desert
            camp
                sagebrush
                    aspen
                        canyon
                            stream . . .

The Chase

Milton's ears twitched as he huddled on the tailgate of the pickup truck. Something inside him grew warm. He could see the pictures the music made. He rubbed his stomach, then washed his whiskers.

"That's beautiful, Dad," said Kathleen. "It reminds me of this place."

"Listen!" whispered Matt.

Above the quiet murmur of the stream, a lonesome howl sounded in the desert night. Milton shivered; hair raised on the back of his neck.

"Coyote," whispered Kathleen.

A chorus of yips and yelps came from another direction.

Milton slowly backed into the deep shadow of the camper doorway.

"Sounds like a coyote party," said Matt.

First one group, then another answered with wailing howls. The coyote calls swept down the mountain side and died away into the distance.

"What a haunting sound," said Mom. The family sat in silence around the fire.

After a moment, Dad said, "Well, this closes our show for the night."

"Already?" asked Matt.

"I don't mind," yawned Kathleen. "I got my wish."

"If we are going to make it home tomorrow, we have a long day ahead. Off to bed with you," Dad stood up. "Matt, here are the keys. Lock up the camper, and I'll put out the fire."

"I sure wish I could find my flashlight," Kathleen headed for the picnic table. "I keep losing it."

Keys jingling, Matt flashed his light toward the camper truck. Milton ducked. Footsteps crunched closer and closer. Milton turned on his tail and slipped through the dark doorway into the camper.

2

Packing Up

KA–LUNK. THUMP. MILTON JERKED awake. Heavy footsteps shook the camper.

"Hand me your sleeping bag," said a muffled voice.

"Matt, spread it on my bunk, would you please?" Kathleen sounded faraway. "And here are new rocks for my collection." She handed up a small bag.

"O.K. You start taking down the pup tent," replied Matt. "I'll be out in a minute."

Deep in the art pack Milton shifted in his nest, listening.

"Here, Matt," came Dad's voice, "this tarp goes in the bottom cupboard."

"And the pup tent will too, right?"

"Yup," said Dad. "and any loose camping gear."

Ka-lunk. Thump. More commotion. Then quiet, no footsteps, the quaking stopped. Milton crept out of the nest he had made in the artist's empty tin water can. He squeezed past the paintbrushes and sketchbook. Light filtered in from under the top flap of the pack, and he peeked out.

Thud. Bump, on the tailgate. Kathleen climbed into the camper.

"Here, Sunrise," crooned Kathleen, laying her Indian doll down on her bunk. "Just rest here on my pillow because we have a long ride through the desert. Tonight I'll tell you another story."

"Hey, Kathleen." Matt sounded close. "Can I trade you comic books? I've read these a million times."

"I guess so," said Kathleen. "Look in my book box."

Matt *flumped* down right next to the art pack. Milton drew back.

"Hey, here's a flashlight," said Matt. "It must be yours."

"Thanks. Are you glad to be going home?" asked Kathleen.

"In a way," said Matt. "I'd stay out here forever if I had a piano with me."

"You miss it?" asked Kathleen.

"Well, yeah, sort of."

"I thought you were sick of it," said Kathleen.

"I said I was tired of practicing," Matt sounded disgusted, "not tired of the piano."

"Sorry, that's just what you said. Don't be mad. Here, have a piece of candy."

"Where did you get that?" asked Matt.

"Shhhh, from Dad."

"Oh, yeah, I won't tell Mom. Bad for the teeth."

"Kathleen," called Dad, "take a walk around camp and pick up any litter. Then see if your Mom needs help closing down the trailer. Matt, let's hitch up."

"Sure thing, Dad," said Matt. "I'll just clear this bunk."

Milton was thrown backwards as the art pack was heaved onto its side. He covered his eyes with his paws, rolled into a ball, and slid back into the tin can. When the pack came to a standstill, he brushed himself off. Everything was sideways. His nest was a jumble of scraps. Uneasy, he nosed forward again, out of the can, and squeezed past the bundle of brushes and the spiral edge of the sketchbook. Suddenly the truck engine roared. *"Help, I'm buzzing all over."* Milton grabbed the sketchbook and hung on.

"Ready?" called Matt from outside.

"Yup," answered Dad from the front seat.

"Come on," called Matt.

Milton poked his nose through the flap, and daylight flooded over him. Blinded, he pulled back, blinking rapidly. The art pack was now close to the end of the bunk, and he could see out the door.

The truck lurched, then moved backwards.

Squinting, Milton peeked out again. He barely made out Matt who stood right outside the open door of the camper and in front of the trailer. Matt waved his hands in the air and motioned one way, then the other, and beckoned to Dad.

Milton looked down. The ground looked a bit fuzzy but he could tell it was sliding by. He covered his eyes with his paws. *"I feel a little dizzy."*

"Whoa! Right over the hitch!" yelled Matt. "On the first try, too!"

Milton retreated into the art pack and crawled back to his tin can. He sighed, picked up tissue scraps, and re-lined the nest. He settled himself in the middle and waited, ears alert.

Footsteps clumped along the aisle. "I finished my job," announced Kathleen. "That's a clean camp."

"Kathleen," called Mom as she climbed into the front seat of the truck. She reached through the opening that connected the front seat of the truck to the interior of the camper. "Push my art pack up here. I think I can pull it through this pass–through window. I want it on the seat beside me in case we stop."

Kathleen shoved the pack through. "It's like a porthole, Mom," she said, "here it comes."

Packing Up

The art pack lurched and jounced, and Milton was again covered with tissue scraps. He held on tight to the can rim. Abruptly the movement stopped.

"Thanks," said Mom.

"*Thanks a lot.*" Milton brushed himself all over. He pushed the scraps back into the can and reshaped his nest again.

"I'm looking for my cap," said Kathleen. "Where did it go? It's my favorite."

"Hey," said Mom. "The granola bar in the map box! Look! Somebody ate a chunk right out of the middle, wrapper and all."

"*Map box?*" Milton licked his lips.

"Looks like a half moon," laughed Kathleen. "It must have been those chipmunks yesterday. One of them was in that box with all the maps and stuff. I chased them out of here about fifteen times. Is my cap in that box?"

Milton blinked.

"Ha-ha," laughed Dad. "That will teach you to leave granola bars all over the place. Who gets the rest of it?"

"Kathleen, your cap is not in the map box," said Mom, "and I'm not going to eat this chewed-up granola bar. It's going into the litter bag."

"*Litter bag?*" Milton sat up. "*What's a litter bag?*"

"I'm ready to leave," said Dad through the window.

"Wait," said Mom, "Let's wash the windshield before we start." The truck door slammed shut.

The front seat was quiet. Milton crawled out of the tin can toward the light. He peeked under the flap and saw two bags. A brown paper sack with the top folded open sat in the map box, alongside the canteen, the maps, a notebook, and a box of tissues. Closer to Milton was an open leather bag. He could dimly make out the brass buckle and a long shoulder strap. The flap was thrown back, and an enticing aroma spoke to him. "*Mmmm, the litter bag.*" He crept out of the art pack, looked this way and that, then dashed around Dad's old hat and leaped for the leather bag. He teetered on the floppy edge. His nose wiggled, twitched, and told him something. *"Mmmm . . . ,"* the delicious scent of granola bar. He dove headfirst into Mom's purse.

The truck door slammed shut. *"'. . . Come, let us haste, the stars grow high,'"* quoted Dad. Another door slammed shut.

"No, they don't," called Kathleen from the back. "It's morning. Do you have a morning poem?"

"Well," Mom's voice sounded close to the purse, "the sun's a star, and it is growing high." The flap on what Milton thought was the litter bag abruptly closed. He blinked in the dark.

"A great day for a trip," said Dad. *"'. . . Come and trip it as you go/On the light fantastic toe!'* Will that do?"

Kathleen giggled.

"Let's go home then," called Matt from the back. "Kathleen, what's this cap doing on my bunk?"

"Oh, thanks," said Kathleen, grabbing her cap and putting it on.

The engine roared, and everything vibrated. Milton tensed in the bottom of Mom's leather purse. The motor hummed, gears shifted, and vibrations continued. After a long while, Milton relaxed. He reached for the granola bar. *"Ah, breakfast."* He tore off the rest of the wrapping and bit hungrily into the delicious feast. *"Mmmm . . . ,"* he sighed, and ignoring the muffled sounds, he ate until he could hold no more. Feeling sleepy, he pushed aside the comb and made a nest out of two old shopping lists and a forgotten tissue. He curled up in his bed and allowed the rhythmic motion of the truck to sweep over him. *"People," he muttered, "live closer than I realized."* He shut his eyes.

3

Stowaway

THE VIBRATIONS STOPPED. MILTON rolled over and yawned. Eyes half–closed he stretched his neck toward the remains of the granola bar. As he chewed he was dimly aware that everything was still. He dozed again. Suddenly with a jolt and a jerk he was in motion, bouncing and bumping around in the bottom of the bag. The comb jabbed into his side as the wallet shifted onto him, squeezing him out of the nest. A tube of lipstick hit him in the ear. He crouched in a corner, barely keeping his nose above the scarf, which threatened to smother him. Wide awake now, he braced his paws against the leather walls and stiffened every muscle.

A door slammed, and the purse *thunked* to a standstill.

"It's always good to be home again," Mom murmured. The top flap lifted, and light poured over Milton. He saw Mom remove her sunglasses, and he wiggled under the scarf. She thrust her eyeglass case into the purse beside the wallet, which crowded Milton even more.

"Oh," she murmured as she closed the flap and picked up her purse. "I must be tired. I thought I saw something move in there." She set it down again. "Wait a minute. I'm not *that* tired."

Light again poured into the purse, and the scarf lifted off Milton. He stared upward, right into Mom's eyes.

"A mouse!" she gasped. "A mouse? In my purse?" The flap was flung across the opening which plunged Milton once more into darkness. He heard Mom shout, "George! Kathleen! Matt! Come quickly! Help!"

Nervously, Milton backed into the corner beside the leftover granola bar. Footsteps pounded closer.

"Help," said Mom again, "I can't believe it, but there's a mouse in my purse!"

"A what?" asked Dad.

"A mouse?" asked Matt, unbelieving.

"Let me see it," cried Kathleen.

"Look there," said Mom. "Look for yourselves."

The flap lifted. Milton froze against the leather as light poured once more into the purse. He stared at another pair of eyes, and then another, and then another pair.

"A mouse," breathed Kathleen.

"A white–footed deer mouse," said Dad.

Milton stared harder.

"Look at those big brown eyes." said Mom, still in shock.

"What is he doing in there?" asked Matt, incredulous.

"My granola bar! Look, the package is half gone."

Dad started chuckling. "How long do you suppose he has been riding around in your purse?"

"A week or so?" giggled Kathleen.

"A month?" snickered Matt.

"I'll never live this down." Mom peered down at Milton and shook her head. "A mouse in my purse. What are we going to do with him?"

"He's mine!" said Matt. "I want him."

"Shouldn't we take him back to his home?" asked Kathleen.

"That's not so easy," said Dad. "Where exactly did he come from? How can we take him back?"

"I cleaned out this purse just a few days ago," said Mom. "There was no mouse then."

"You mean you baited this mouse trap?" teased Matt.

"I warned you about leaving granola bars everywhere," laughed Dad. "I don't think it was chipmunks in the truck."

Kathleen said, "You can have him, Matt. You are the one who loves wild animals. And anyway, I love Bertha, and she loves me."

"I'll take good care of him," replied Matt. "That old aquarium might work until we fix up a cage."

"Wait a minute," said Mom. "Don't deer mice make people sick from some virus?"

"Well," said Dad, "some mice might carry hantavirus if they are overpopulated and if the burrows are full of mouse droppings. Mice do make good pets though if we give them the right care."

"*A clean burrow,*" muttered Milton. "*My mama taught me.*"

"He's a wild mouse," said Matt. "Will he be happy in a cage?"

"Well, Son, mice are pretty adaptable. I know some people have them for pets. How do we tell if a mouse is happy? Hard to know, but just think, this mouse probably found us by that stream in Nevada. We camped there for ten days, and it was good animal habitat. Somehow he managed to get into the camper."

"I never left my purse sitting outdoors," said Mom. "Even if we drove back four hundred miles across the Great Basin Desert, isn't it already too late?"

"Too late for what?" asked Kathleen.

"*Too late?*" Milton squirmed in the purse.

"Too late for him to get his own place back," answered Dad. "The minute he abandoned his territory, another mouse would have moved right in."

"*Or a packrat.*" Milton hunkered down behind the wallet. "*I won't go back there.*"

"Now he is the outsider, and the defender on its home territory will always fight harder," said Dad.

"What would happen to him?" asked Kathleen.

Milton tried to think of another good place. *"Too far from the creek. Not much food on that hill. No place to hide."*

"Life would get pretty hard for him. He probably wouldn't survive here either if we turn him loose. This is not quite his habitat."

"You mean he wouldn't have enough to eat?" asked Kathleen. "Perhaps not."

"Would our cat get him?" she asked. "Bertha is a great hunter."

"Well, all cats eat mice if they can catch them."

Milton shuddered. He had seen a bobcat once.

"Well," said Mom. "He picked us. Even so, I'm not sure we should keep him."

"He needs a clean cage and a good diet, and we will be okay. Pet Shops sell mice for pets. Matt, don't pick him up with your bare hands," said Dad. "Let's get him into a cage. I hate to leave him in a dangerous place. Life is a miracle, even mouse life."

"O.K., Dad," said Matt. "I'll go find that old aquarium. It has a lid."

"Be sure that lid is tight. Deer mice can jump straight up in the air two feet or more."

The flap closed. Milton was grateful. The darkness gave him a few moments to think. He crept along the bottom of the purse, around the wallet and past the comb. No place to hide; no place to run; no hole to creep into.

A *clunk* sounded beside the purse, and Matt said, "Here's this old aquarium. He can't get out of this. I put in a little flower pot and turned it over for a hiding place. He can go in and out the hole."

Light streamed into the purse. A gloved hand reached down and began removing things, first the eyeglass case, then the scarf. Milton made himself as small as possible.

"There now," Matt talked softly to him. "Don't be afraid. You can make a secret hideaway in this little flower pot, and I'll find another granola bar just for you."

Milton looked about anxiously. The purse lurched. The whole world went sideways, then upside–down. Milton slipped and slid, clutching at the leather. In a *swoosh* of tissue pieces, a paper clip, and granola crumbs, he tumbled out of the purse and landed with a *flump* in sawdust.

"*Come let us haste.*" Milton scrambled to his feet, leaped onto the flower pot, and vaulted upward just as Matt was setting the wire lid. Mouse paws grabbed the top rim of the aquarium. Milton pushed his head through the gap under the closing lid and squeezed his small body through. He sprang to the floor, ears flat, and tail flying.

"There he goes!" yelled Matt.

"Under the couch!" cried Kathleen.

"We can't have a mouse loose in the house," said Mom. "They chew on things."

"Don't worry," said Dad. "We'll catch him."

Milton dashed under the couch to the back wall, then along the wall to the bookcase. As hands and a broom reached under the couch, he hopped into the bottom shelf of the bookcase and slipped behind a couple of books. He crouched low, panting for breath.

"He's mine," said Matt, shaking the broom.

"Mice get into things." Mom threw her hands in the air and declared, "They are not clean."

"He's gone," Kathleen wailed, "what should we do?"

Dad frowned. "We'll think of something."

4

Water

MILTON SNOOZED OFF AND on all day until at last the family went to bed. It was time for him to get up, and he was ready for breakfast. He peeked over the books. No one stirred. He crept around the books, scampered across the rug, and climbed the sofa. His stomach growled. He hopped onto the coffee table and nosed around magazines and a large book. He sniffed the empty coffee cup. Nothing to eat. He jumped off the table and darted toward the kitchen. At the doorway, he paused. His nose wiggled, twitched, and told him something. He dashed under the table and scooped supper crumbs into his cheek pouches, then he retreated under a cabinet where he nibbled daintily on his breakfast.

After washing his whiskers he looked about. *"The creek? I'm thirsty. Where is the creek?"*

He scampered across the kitchen and into the hallway. No creek. He thought for a moment. *"The map box . . . the leaky canteen."* He sniffed his way down the hallway and slipped into a pink bedroom.

He climbed up drawers to the top of the dresser. Curious, he sniffed around the perfume bottle. *"Mmmm, smells like flowers."* When Milton came to a small pile of smooth rocks, he paused; they smelled like home. He closed his eyes and could see his nest by the rose bushes, the rushing creek. He was still thirsty. He scrambled down to the floor and explored under the bed. Nothing to eat, nothing to drink. He climbed up the bedspread and crept across the lumpy blanket. From here he could see out Kathleen's window where the moon shone in the night sky. He watched the moon through the window as he crept toward the head of the bed. He quietly climbed onto Kathleen's pillow. The moon made him want to sing. Forgetting where he was, he trilled a little mouse trill close to Kathleen's ear. When she rolled over in bed, he somersaulted to the floor and scurried to the door.

He looked to the left, then to the right. Homesick, the mouse sighed deeply, then blinked. Water, he smelled water. He followed his nose down the hall and into Mom and Dad's bedroom. The scent of water led him to a smaller room, and the door stood open. He stepped onto the smooth floor.

Milton circled the small room, sniffing. He bumped his nose against a cold, round, white tower. *"Water!"* In blink time Milton leaped straight up and grabbed the edge of the toilet. He scrambled up and teetered on the ledge. *"A pond!"* He slipped. Paws flailing, Milton fell into the water with a *splash!* He popped up to the surface, spluttering and sneezing. *"Can't touch."* He gasped and thrashed around the small pool, trying to keep his chin above water. He mouse-paddled until one paw touched down.

"The shallow end." Relieved and gulping for air, Milton steadied himself on the slippery bottom.

He heard a soft footstep, a click, and the overhead light flashed on. He hunkered down into the water and looked up into Mom's startled face.

"I heard something splash all right. You look half-drowned." She called, "George, wake up! Get Matt. I found our runaway mouse."

Milton's paws slipped out from under him. He spluttered to the surface. *"Slick bedrock. Can't climb out of here."*

More footsteps, then a deep chuckle, and Milton looked up.

"A wet mouse," laughed Dad. "'. . . But fie my wandering mouse/How thou dost stray!'"

"No dear," said Mom, "the poem says "muse," 'but fie my wandering muse', not mouse."

"Well," said Dad, "That too."

Get me out of here. Milton was cold, wet, and miserable.

Matt appeared, yawning. "Oh, good," he said, rubbing his eyes. "I thought you might be lost forever."

Milton heard Kathleen's slippers scuff into the room. "What's going on?" she asked, half asleep.

"It's the mouse. He fell into the toilet," said Mom.

Dad spoke up. "Let's put him in that old hamster cage until we can make him a better one. He can't get out of that."

"O.K., Dad," said Matt, "but first I'm going to get those thick work gloves. I don't want him to bite me."

Matt disappeared. Milton waited, afraid to move. A jump was impossible; he shivered. Moments later, there was a *whomp*, as Matt set down the empty cage.

"Close the door in case he gets loose again." said Dad. "Mom, you and Kathleen wait in the bedroom. It's crowded in here."

Matt's face was framed in the white circle as a large gloved hand slowly reached down toward Milton. Rough leather fingers spread out and scooped him up. The leather closed around him tighter and tighter, and he was gently lifted out of the water. Milton panicked. He wiggled and squirmed with all his might. Matt reached in with his other hand to get a better hold, the gloves slipped, and Milton splashed back into the water! He gulped and spit and sneezed while he thrashed around. He frantically mouse–paddled toward the shallow end. The gloved hand reached down again. This time Matt scooped him up and held on tight.

Milton squeaked. *Get me out of here!*

Just as the glove cleared the toilet seat, he wiggled free and sprang into the air.

"There he goes!" cried Dad.

"Get him!" yelled Matt.

"What's happening?" called Mom from the other side of the door.

In the bathroom Milton ran wildly back and forth across the floor, around the shuffling feet and reaching hands. He zoomed along the edge of the wall and under the cabinet overhang. Suddenly he spied a dark hole underneath the bottom drawer and dived into it.

"He's gone!" wailed Matt.

"He can't be!" cried Dad.

"What?" called Mom.

Milton scrambled under the drawer and climbed up onto the back of it.

"Pull out that drawer," ordered Dad. "Maybe we can reach him."

As the drawer moved, Milton snatched at the board above him and scrambled up onto the next drawer.

"Take it clear out," said Dad, "and set it on the floor."

"I don't see him, Dad," said Matt. "I'll take out the next one too."

Milton clambered up all four drawers, one after the other. In the dim light he spotted a small hole under the end of the counter top. He hopped into it and hid there, panting.

"I still can't see anything moving in there," said Matt. "Where did he go?"

Milton shivered.

"I give up," said Dad.

"What happened?" said Mom, opening the door.

"He disappeared," said Dad, unbelieving, "into the woodwork."

"What are you going to do?"

"I'm going to get the mouse trap," said Dad, darkly.

"Not that," said Kathleen.

Milton trembled.

"Oh, no, Dad," said Matt. "Let's try to catch him alive. He will make a great pet. Don't we still have that live-animal trap in the shed?"

"Yes, I suppose we could try that," said Dad. "but it's a pretty big trap for such a small mouse."

"I'll go find it now," Matt turned to go.

"I think it can wait till morning," said Mom. "Put the drawers back in. We'll just close this bathroom door so that he can't go anywhere else tonight. We can use the other bathroom."

Milton waited, listening, until everyone had gone back to bed. Then he hopped into the top drawer and shook himself. Water drops flew every direction. He wiped down his fur with his paws. He rubbed his coat and preened himself. When he was dry and had stopped shivering, he crept past a hairbrush and Dad's razor case. His stomach growled.

"*But fie my wandering mouse . . . ,*" he echoed and climbed over the back side of the drawer. He dropped from drawer to drawer until he reached the bottom and peeped out the hole. All was quiet. "*. . . How thou dost stray!*" Milton crept softly forward and squeezed under the bathroom door.

5

Runaway

"WE CAN'T HAVE A mouse loose in the house," said Mom. "He'll chew on things." She put another piece of bread into the toaster.

Under the refrigerator Milton sleepily lifted his head. He blinked his eyes, then snuggled into his nest again.

Dad put down the morning paper. "Matt's getting the trap right now," he said.

"Did anything happen after I went to bed?" asked Kathleen.

Matt stomped into the kitchen and set down the trap with a *bang*.

Milton jerked awake.

"Here it is," said Matt, "but isn't this too big for a mouse? It's big enough for a raccoon."

"Probably," said Dad, "but it's all we have, and it might work."

Milton yawned. *"Noisy in here."*

"We think that mouse is loose in the house," Mom explained to Kathleen. "He certainly is not in the bathroom." She reached into a drawer. "Oh no!" she said. "That mouse has been in the kitchen!" She pulled out another drawer. "Here too! This is terrible." She opened drawer after drawer. "That mouse left his calling card in nearly every drawer in the kitchen."

"Let me see," said Kathleen. "What's a calling card?"

"Mouse droppings," said Mom, exasperated.

"Is that what that is?!" exclaimed Kathleen. "He left his calling card on my pillow, too."

Dad laughed out loud. "Well, that just goes to show he gets around."

"I thought I heard a little squeal too, but when I sat up in bed I couldn't see anything."

"Did it sound like a little trill?" asked Dad.

"Maybe," said Kathleen, "but I was half asleep."

"'. . . and sweetly singing round about thy bed, Strew all [his] blessings round about thy sleeping head?'" intoned Dad. "Deer mice have a little secret: they 'sing', but I've never heard one. I read it's like a very faint trilling sound. I wish I could hear one sometime, but I'm never that close to a mouse."

"A secret?" Kathleen reached for some toast. "A singing mouse?"

"*Of course*," chittered Milton, turning around in his nest.

"Amazing," said Mom.

"*It's hard to get any sleep around here.*" Milton resettled himself.

"He must be in the kitchen," said Dad. "This is where the food is. Let's put the trap in here."

"What a mess," said Mom. "Now I'll have to clean out all these drawers."

"I'll help you, Mom." Kathleen opened the peanut butter.

"I suppose we should wear rubber gloves," said Mom. "I'm still not sure about the hantavirus."

"What should we bait the trap with?" asked Matt.

"Mice are seedeaters, but I don't think we have any seeds. How about a bit of peanut butter," said Dad. "A mouse can't resist that."

Milton licked his lips.

"That's what I'm putting on my toast," said Kathleen. "Here, have some."

With a table knife Matt scooped a bit of peanut butter, spread it on a small cracker, and placed the cracker on the bait platform in the trap. "That ought to do it," he said. "I'll set the trap right here beside the refrigerator."

Milton lifted his nose, sniffing.

Dad set down his coffee cup, and quoted: "'. . . and, if it happen as I did forecast,/The daintiest dishes shall be served up last.'"

"Is that your friend again?" asked Kathleen.

"Bertha! Get out of there!" yelled Matt. "Kathleen, get your cat! Keep her away from that trap!"

Milton froze, whiskers quivering.

"John Milton, my hero," answered Dad. "He had a line for everything. He was blind you know."

"How could he write poetry if he was blind?" said Kathleen, as she picked up Bertha.

"He was a true overcomer," said Dad. "John thought up his lines and spoke them, and he had a helper who wrote down every word."

"Wow," said Kathleen. "That's amazing." She carried Bertha into the living room. "I'll put her outside. Come on, Bertha." She hugged the cat and stroked her fur.

Milton slumped in his nest. *Cats are dangerous!*

"That trap is so large," said Dad. "I'll run down to the neighbor's. John is a biologist, and he may have a smaller one."

Milton listened as Dad's footsteps faded away. Drawers opened and shut. Kathleen chattered while she and Mom cleaned them out. There was a clatter of dishes in the sink as Matt loaded the dishwasher. The hum of activity became a blur of sound. Milton yawned, then closed his eyes and drifted off to sleep again.

He woke much later. Soft piano notes sounded from the living room, sending fragments of melody throughout the house. *What's that?* Milton's sensitive ears quivered as Matt's fingers reached for the notes of Beethoven's *Für Elise*. The melody rippled through the air. Entranced, Milton sat in his nest and felt a spot in his middle grow warm. He rubbed his stomach. He had never heard anything so beautiful.

Footsteps thumped across the kitchen. "Here's the smaller trap," said Dad. "I've never seen such a small live–animal trap. It's mouse size. This one is more likely to work."

Milton crept out of his nest and sniffed along the bottom of the refrigerator. He peeked through the grate.

Matt came from the living room. "O.K., Dad," he said. He moved the peanut butter bait from the large trap to the smaller trap.

"That Beethoven was sounding pretty good when I came in," said Dad. "I think you may have a gift there, Matt."

Milton paced back and forth.

"Thanks, Dad. I really missed the piano when we were camping these past weeks. It made me want to play."

"Really?" said Dad. "You mean you really want to be good?"

"Yes," said Matt, working on the trap.

Milton's nose wiggled. He could smell the peanut butter.

"Well, it's a lot of work. I guess you know that," said Dad. "If you are willing to put in the practice time, we'll find you the best teacher in town. Is that what you want?"

"Yup, and the mouse. I want that mouse too," grinned Matt.

"Maybe we should go look up phone numbers," said Dad, "and get some recommendations."

"Good idea," replied Matt. "I know a couple of names already. Grab your hat. I'll tell you what I know while we go hunt for the lizard I saw out back yesterday."

"Okay," said Dad, reaching for his hat.

Milton watched their shoes grow smaller as they walked toward the door. When they were gone, he crept out from under the refrigerator and sniffed his way across the floor to the small wire box. He nosed all around the trap, then reached in, carefully pulled the bait cracker off the trigger platform, and backed away from the trap. He licked the peanut butter, then nibbled, and spat it out. *"Sticky, yuk."*

He dashed under the kitchen table; not many crumbs left after Kathleen swept the floor. He darted across the room, ducking behind furniture. He dashed down the hallway and turned the corner into the first bedroom. He flew around a pile of dirty clothes, past some old sneakers, and over a pair of roller blades. Milton slipped under the bed.

Late that evening Milton awakened in the nest he had made in an old sock. His ears quivered. He heard a most beautiful sound. It was bigger than a bird song, richer than the tumbling creek at home, fuller than a cricket chirp, more tuneful than the wind in the aspens. A tapestry of tones filled the starlit corners of Matt's bedroom, as slowly measured notes of the *Moonlight Sonata* played from Matt's small stereo. The calm beauty of the first part flowed into a charming second part. Then the music thundered with an exciting gallop of color and movement. Milton sat up straight; the music was too exciting for him to hold still. He popped out of the sock with his tail swishing, peeked over a shoebox, and began to run in circles under the bed.

Matt lay in bed, listening. "Someday I'll play like that," he moved his fingers over the blanket like it was a keyboard.

The music stopped. Milton collapsed, puffing. A great silence lay over the house. After a time, Milton wiggled his nose; his empty stomach spoke to him. He crept forward, sniffing in the dark. It was time for a mouse breakfast. He picked up a dried apple core and dashed back to his nest. He nibbled daintily, then washed and smoothed his whiskers. He was still hungry. Dad's words echoed in his ears, *" . . . the daintiest dishes will be served up last."* He darted across the room, squeezed under the door, and headed down the hallway.

6

The Cat

MILTON ROUNDED THE DOOR jamb. He looked right and left, but no one stirred. He hugged close to the baseboard and trotted into the kitchen. He paused once and looked over his shoulder. Not a sound. No movement. His stomach growled, and he moved on.

Mee-owwwww! He froze in his tracks. From outside the house came the raucous sound of cat. The hair on the back of his neck raised. *Mee-owww! Mee-owww!*

Down the hallway, a door opened. Milton dived for cover under the refrigerator. Footsteps padded into the living room, and the front door creaked.

Kathleen whispered, "Bertha! What do you have there? I know you caught something." There was a small *meow*, and a light came on. "Oh no, you caught a mouse!"

Just then Matt shuffled into the living room. "What is it?" he asked, sleepily.

"Bertha caught a mouse," said Kathleen.

"A deer mouse," said Matt. "Look at the white belly. Oh, I hope that wasn't our mouse."

"How could it be? Bertha is outside."

Dad's slippers scuffed along the hallway. "Another mouse?" he asked. "Well, that's the way cats do, whether we like it or not." Dad looked the mouse over. "It has to be a different species than our Great Basin mouse. The color is not quite the same; this one is a little darker. There are lots of different species, but they look very much alike."

"Well, eat it up, Bertha," said Matt. "Then we'd better bring her inside."

"Ewww," said Kathleen, "I wish she would hurry up. I can't watch."

"Well, her catch isn't wasted," said Dad. "Now back to bed. Morning will be here all too soon." His voice dropped to a dramatic whisper, "'. . . thus done the tales, to bed they creep,/By whispering winds soon lulled asleep.'"

"Oh, Dad," said Kathleen, scooping up Bertha.

"Just be sure to close your door," said Matt. "We want to catch our own deer mouse."

Slippers scuffed down the hallway, doors closed, and the house grew quiet. Milton waited a long time before he crept out from under the refrigerator, past the wire trap, and nosed around under the kitchen table. He found a few crumbs and ate them on the spot, then washed his whiskers.

Feeling safer, he darted into the living room, ran past the piano, and squeezed under the stereo cabinet. Behind the stereo he wiggled through a maze of cords and wires and crawled into the back holes of the cabinet one by one. No place for a nest. He emerged from the last hole a little breathless from dust. "*Aah-choo!*" He sneezed and brushed his nose with his paws.

A muffled *swish* down the hallway made him sit up. Nothing more, but he waited. All was quiet until his stomach growled. He crept around the stereo and under the old Morris chair. He sniffed around the carved claw foot. His nose wiggled, twitched, and told him something. "*I smell something delicious.*" He spied a white, puffy morsel and pounced on it. He nibbled the puff part then spat out the remainder. "*Nothing there,*" he thought, and dropped the popcorn kernel. He eyed the distance up to the seat cushion, then leaped. In mid–air he caught another scent, animal scent. The cat! He landed on the seat cushion for one brief gasp, long enough to glimpse a rising mass of fur, whiskers, and sharp teeth!

"*Yikes!*" he squeaked.

The cat struck with open claws, and Milton flew off the cushion. He tumbled head over paws onto the floor and scrambled underneath the big chair. In a wink he was out the other side and zooming across the room. The cat bounded after him in great leaps.

Milton looked frantically for a hiding hole as he streaked along. Just past the piano bench a shape loomed in his path. He checked his stride and scrambled up the side of an antique woven–wicker wine bottle that sat near the hearth. He climbed the wicker, spiraling around to the back, up the far side, and onto the bottle-neck where a hole opened invitingly.

He heard the horrible swish of cat at full speed. For a split second he hesitated, but terrified of oncoming claws, he dove through the hole into the bottle and plunged to the bottom. *Thunk!*

He lay there panting for a moment, then sprang to his feet. He ran around and around the smooth glass bottom. "*Safe.*" A furry paw reached down into the neck of the bottle. A mean eye glared at him. "*Go away,*" he squeaked.

Bertha circled the bottle, staring between slits in the wicker. She growled. Milton waited and waited until the cat finally slunk away. Milton heard one disgusted *Mee-owww* before Bertha rounded the corner and disappeared down the hallway.

A moment later Milton heard a bedroom door open and a swish of slipper on the rug.

"Bertha, you're not supposed to be in here," hissed Matt. He scooped her up in his arms. "You're going back outside."

The Cat

Milton watched Matt carry the cat to the door and put her out. *"Good riddance."* Milton sat back on his haunches. He smoothed his fur, then brushed his ears, and preened his whiskers. He paced once more around the bottle. *"Now to get out of here."*

Kathleen's slippers shuffled past the bottle. "What happened?"

Matt hissed, "Bertha got out."

Kathleen whispered, "I thought I had my door shut. I guess it didn't catch. I'm sorry."

"She probably ate my mouse," said Matt sternly.

"Here I am." Milton crept around the inside of the bottle and peeked through a crack in the wickerwork.

Matt scuffed past in his pajamas and went toward the kitchen. Milton heard the scrape of metal on metal, then Matt's whisper. "He's not in the trap. Bertha's in big trouble, and so are you!"

Kathleen sniffled. "I'm sorry. I guess Bertha knows how to get out of my room. I'm going back to bed." Her footsteps faded down the hall, and a door shut quietly.

Milton leaped straight up, but the smooth glass curved inward. He could not get a grip on anything. He leaped again and fell back, then paced around the bottom circle of glass. There was no way out; his ears drooped. *"Trapped."*

Matt came back into the living room. He flopped down on his stomach and looked under the sofa. He wiggled over to the bookcase and poked around the books. Matt looked behind the stereo set and finally sighed. He pulled back the drapery at the deck door and stood for a long moment in the half–glow of the coming sunrise. "Milton, where are you?" he whispered.

"In here." Milton paced back and forth on the cold glass.

Matt dropped the curtain and again scuffed past the bottle.

"Save me." Milton pressed his nose against the glass, but Matt disappeared down the hallway. Milton sighed, *"'. . . thus done the tales, to bed they creep . . . '"* He slumped tiredly against the side of the bottle.

7

Saved

PIANO MUSIC AGAIN WOKE Milton. He peeked through the wicker and watched Matt's hands move over the keyboard. He closed his eyes. The music carried his thoughts away from the cold, hard prison of the bottle. He remembered his home in the desert canyon and how the wind fluttered the aspen leaves. Muffled footsteps interrupted his reverie. Milton blinked and focused on Kathleen's sneakers. The music stopped.

"Matt, I'm sorry about Bertha," said Kathleen.

"Oh, that's O.K.," said Matt. "I was a little upset in the night. I'm sorry I was cross. We may still find Milton the mouse. Who knows? He could be anywhere."

"Milton the mouse?" echoed Kathleen. "Did you give him a name?"

Milton lifted his ears.

"Yup," said Matt.

Milton was pleased. *A good name,* he murmured, *just right.*

"Why Milton?" asked Kathleen.

"It fits," said Matt. "Just like the poem says: he has fantastic toes, he wanders, we want him in captivity . . . ."

Milton looked at his toes. *Fantastic?* He stared through the wavy glass.

"Jody is coming over to play today. Maybe we can all look for the mouse."

"Good idea," said Matt.

Milton paced around the glass bottom, and his stomach growled.

Kathleen walked away, and the piano music started again. Milton covered his eyes with his paws to keep out the light. He wiggled and squirmed but could not find a comfortable position. With no nest, no tissues to warm him, the cold of the glass seeped through his fur. He lay there listening until he finally dozed off.

Much later running footsteps awakened Milton.

"Come on, Jody!" exclaimed Kathleen. "We'll play in here."

"It's so hot outside today," said a new voice.

Milton watched a pair of red sneakers walk past the bottle.

"What should we play?" asked Jody.

"Do you like to play Treasure Hunt?" asked Kathleen.

"Oh, that's fun."

"We'll need Matt. I'll go get him." Kathleen's sneakers tromped past. "Matt! Come here!"

Milton watched from behind the glass wall. Where was his dark, cozy burrow?

Matt answered from down the hall, "What do you want?"

"*I want to go home.*" Milton sighed.

"Jody's here, and we want to play Treasure Hunt," said Kathleen. "Will you help us?"

Matt sauntered into the living room. "You mean you want me to hide a treasure and write some clues for you to find?" he asked.

"Yes," said Jody. "You're so good at it."

Matt frowned. "That's not hunting for the mouse."

"The what?" asked Jody.

"Oh please, Matt," said Kathleen. "We can't hide the clues if we are supposed to find them."

"It's a good day for lizard hunting. I was planning to go look for one," said Matt.

"Oh no," said Kathleen, "it's too hot to out there. Come on. Write the clues and hide the notes. Then Jody and I will hunt," said Kathleen. "Please, Matt? Then we can all look for the mouse." She turned to Jody, "We lost a mouse," she said.

"A mouse?" said Jody.

"OK," said Matt finally. "You two go somewhere else."

"Oh, good!" Kathleen jumped up and grabbed Jody's arm. "Come to my room, Jody. I'll tell you all about it. Call us when you're ready, Matt."

The girls giggled and ran down the hallway.

Matt disappeared into the kitchen. He returned with a short stick in one hand and something in the other. *"Are those cookies?"* Milton sat up and stared through the wavy glass of the old bottle. His mouth watered.

Matt went to the coffee table where he lifted the lid of a fancy box sitting there. A tinkling tune began to play. He grabbed the catch and turned off the music, then plopped the cookies into the music box and shut the lid.

"I hope they didn't hear that," Matt muttered. He reached into his back pocket and pulled out small sheets of writing paper. He sat down on the sofa, leaned over the coffee table, and moved the stick over the white paper.

Milton saw him fold up one piece of paper, then another. Matt pushed one folded paper down into the crack between the sofa cushions. The others he hid around the room.

Matt came over and stood beside the bottle. Milton looked at frayed tennis shoes with floppy laces. He stared at the worn cuffs of Matt's jeans. He ran back and forth in the bottle. *"Help, get me out of here."* Panting, he lay down again and closed his eyes. He could picture the cold spring that bubbled up beside his old camp burrow. He licked his lips.

"O.K." yelled Matt. "Come out. I'm ready!"

A door burst open, and the girls hurried into the room.

"Where do we start?" asked Kathleen. "This will be fun."

"Right here," answered Matt, handing her the first piece of paper.

Jody looked over Kathleen's shoulder. She thought for a minute, then said, "I know where that clue is." She ran over to the sofa and reached down between the cushions and pulled out the next note.

"Hah!" cried Kathleen. "That one was easy! What does this note say?"

"Get me out of here." Milton pressed his nose to the glass.

The girls searched the room, finding first one note, then another.

"I can't wait to see what the treasure is," cried Jody jumping up and down in excitement.

"Water," Milton paced around the circle, *"food, and running loose."*

The girls pulled books out of the bookcase and found the next clue.

"That's No. 10," said Matt. "That's the last clue."

"Read it, Jody," said Kathleen.

"All right. It says:

'Maybe it 'tis,
Maybe it 'tisn't,
If your tune's in a bucket,
A basket it isn't.'"

"What could that mean?" asked Kathleen.

"If you don't find it," said Matt, "I get all the treasure."

"It must be something to eat," said Kathleen.

"Let me out." Milton's stomach growled. *"I can run and hide. I can find a mouse hole. I can make a home."* He pressed his nose against the glass again.

"Tune has something to do with music," said Jody. The girls looked in the piano and then through the music on the shelf.

Kathleen stubbed her toe on the woven–wicker bottle. Milton rocked slightly, sliding on the glass.

"Look at that," she said. "That looks like a basket, but it isn't." She reached for the bottle.

Milton's feet slipped out from under him as the bottle lifted and swayed. Flat on his back he saw a surprised blue eye stare down at him through the hole.

"A mouse!" shrieked Kathleen and dropped the bottle.

Milton bounced. *"Ouch!"*

"A mouse?" asked Matt. "Let me see!"

Milton felt weak and dizzy. He rolled over onto his paws as the bottle was lifted again. Another blue eye stared at him from above.

"It's Milton!" yelled Matt. "Whoopee!"

"Hurray!" shouted Kathleen. "I found him!"

"Hurray," echoed Milton and rubbed his head with his paws.

"Is Milton his name?" asked Jody.

"Yup," said Matt.

Milton steadied himself against the side as Matt gently set the bottle down on the carpet.

"Did you say mouse?" asked Mom as she came into the room.

"You'll never believe this!" said Matt. "Look what's inside the old bottle."

"I'm going to tell Dad," said Kathleen, running out of the room.

Milton saw another blue eye peeking at him. Mom laughed. "I'm certainly glad to see you," she said. "Looks like you trapped yourself!"

Milton waited nervously.

"How are you going to get him out of there?" Mom stood up.

"I have an idea," said Matt. "You watch him. I'll be right back."

"Ho there!" boomed Dad bursting through the front door with Kathleen at his heels. "So we finally caught the runaway." He reached for the bottle. "Now there's a real mouse trap."

Milton slipped on the glass as the bottle rose in the air again. He saw Dad peering through the wicker.

"'. . . Held with his melodious harmony/In willing chains and sweet captivity,'" recited Dad. "Well, maybe not too willing, but there he is."

"Here," Matt *clumped* into the room with a deep wastebasket. "Let's try this."

"That's a pretty big container," said Dad.

"It's too tall for him to jump out," answered Matt.

Milton sideslipped and rolled as the bottle lifted and tipped sideways. Wildly grabbing at air, he slid toward the neck of the bottle. Frightened, he stiffened all four legs and tail; he slid to a halt. *"Whoa."* He looked down through the opening. A cavernous space yawned beneath him.

"He won't come out," said Kathleen.

"Shake the bottle," said Dad.

"Come on, Milton," coaxed Matt.

"Not me, too dangerous," Milton mumbled. He braced his tail against the glass.

"Such histrionics!" said Dad. "He probably can recite poetry too."

"Here, Dad," said Matt. "Hold him upright and watch him for a minute. I have another idea."

Moments later, the bottle tipped again. Milton slid to the neck and looked out. This time he was looking at sawdust. He sniffed. He could smell the clean, wood smell, and something else. Water. He licked his lips.

"Now everybody, back away," said Matt. "Leave him alone for a bit. He may come out by himself."

Milton's nose wiggled. His nose twitched. His nose told him something: *"Granola bar!"* He relaxed his front paws and slid nose first down the bottleneck to the opening and paused. "'. . . *In willing chains, and sweet captivity . . .' at least for now."* He looked at the sawdust and gulped, then took a deep breath and slipped out of the bottle.

8

Settling In

"THE CAGE IS READY, but I can't figure out how to move him into it," said Matt. "If I give him the chance, he's going to run."

Milton cracked open another sunflower seed. *"You bet,"* he muttered.

"Yes," said Kathleen, "and he'll head for the nearest hiding place, especially if it's a hole."

"Holes are best," thought Milton, nibbling.

"A hole," said Matt. "Hmmm. That gives me an idea." He crawled partway under his bed and came up holding a tennis ball can.

"What do you see?" he asked Kathleen.

Kathleen rolled her eyes. "I see an empty tennis ball can."

"I see a hole," said Matt, "a large hole, maybe too large, but it's a hole. And it has a lid." Matt dropped a few sunflower seeds into the can.

"Brilliant," said Kathleen. "Let's see if it works."

Matt gently lowered the tennis ball can to the bottom of the wastebasket. Milton stopped nibbling and looked at the big hole. Curious, he crept toward the can and sniffed around the opening. He loved holes. He licked the cool metal. He touched it with one paw, sniffed again, then slowly, slowly tiptoed into the can.

"Bingo," whispered Matt and slipped the lid over the can opening. "I've got him." He lifted the can out of the wastebasket and up to the open cage door. He quickly removed the lid, then pushed the can into the cage and closed the door. Milton stuffed his cheek pouch with sunflower seeds and crept out of the can. *"Mmmmm, this must be paradise,"* he murmured, *"a home, food, water."*

He headed for the corner and buried seeds in the sawdust. He hopped onto the upside–down flower pot and popped into the hole. He peeked out from under the bottom rim, then disappeared underneath where he made a nest out of the sawdust. While the mouse was busy, Matt pulled the can out of the cage.

"I didn't think it would work," said Kathleen. "But look at that."

"He should be happy for a while," said Matt, satisfied. "I'm going to go practice."

~~~

And so the days rolled by. Milton ran in his wheel at night and slept most of the day. When Matt came to bed, Milton waited for him to push the stereo button to start the bedtime music. It worked every time. Sometimes the music tickled his toes; sometimes it set him to dreaming; but always it warmed his stomach and filled an empty spot inside. When the music flowed over the room he felt at home. He felt so much at home that he hummed along to the music, and sometimes in the night he sang to himself, a small squeaky trill.

One day Kathleen was in Matt's room. "I think I will make up a song about Milton," she said.

"Really?" scoffed Matt. "Are you a composer?"

"I can hear it in my head already." She got up to leave.

"That's what Beethoven did," said Matt. "He became deaf. He could hear the music in his head. He wrote the notes down, but he was never able to hear what it sounded like."

"Wow," said Kathleen. "That's amazing, kind of like John Milton, the poet, who was blind and couldn't read his own writing. I'm not deaf. I can hear my song, but mine is simple. Beethoven wrote a million notes in his music."

"Yup," said Matthew, "and I'm trying to learn a few thousand of them."

"Well," said Kathleen, "if you manage to memorize those pieces that's a big accomplishment."

"Right," said Matt, "and then not be too scared to play them for the concert."

"Are you scared to play in the recital?" asked Kathleen.

"Well, sure," said Matt. "Somehow I have to overcome that, and not just play the notes, but do a good job of it."

"You'll be okay," said Kathleen. "I'm sure you'll figure out how to do that."

"I'm working on it," said Matt.

"Did you ever think of taking Milton with you when you practice?"

"You mean, cage and all?" asked Matt.

"Sure. He's a musical mouse. He woke me up that night."

"Hmmm. It might be okay." Matt grabbed the wire handle and carried the cage into the living room. He set it down right beside the piano bench. "Except for Bertha," he said.

"I'll grab the cat. She doesn't need to be in here." Kathleen scooped up Bertha and walked out humming.

Milton hunkered down in his nest. He had been up all night running in his wheel. He was a little sleepy, but when the piano music started, he sat up. He pointed his ears toward the sound and listened. Matt ran scales up and down the keyboard at first, but then he started to play an energetic tune, a Beethoven *Contra Dance*. Milton felt the rhythm all the way from the top of his head to his toes. Pretty soon he was out from under the flower pot and hopping around. He could not stay still. He even hopped into his wheel and ran for a bit.

Matt noticed the wheel going around and laughed. "You like this *Contra Dance*, do you? I'll play it again." And he did. After that he worked on the first part of the *Moonlight Sonata*, and Milton crept back into his nest. The soft harmonies flowed over him. He closed his eyes and went to sleep dreaming about his old home by the creek and the moon rising over the desert mountains.

For a time Milton was content to dream, to have a wheel for running, food that was easy to get, and always a supply of water. He was warm and dry and fed and watered, and he loved the music. What more could he want?

A day came, however, when Milton peeked out from under the flower pot, looked past the cage wires, and wished for his old burrow. Or maybe he could make a new one in the rocks. He wanted to run free. He hankered to explore trails, find where his cousins lived, eat ripe berries off the Oregon Grape  shrubs, and lick water right out of the creek. "*This cage life is good,*" he sighed; but it was not the wild life, romping through weeds, stealing food, running from danger, even the packrat. He stared into space, remembering.

On cage cleaning day Matt came along with the tennis ball can. As he carefully opened the door, he started talking to Milton. "You know what Milton? I'm going to play in a recital next month. My teacher said I can do the first movement of the *Moonlight Sonata*. Won't that be great? She says I'm ready. I love Beethoven," he said.

"*So do I,*" agreed Milton, on alert as he watched the cage door open.

"Matt! You've got to come and see this!" Kathleen burst into the room and crashed right into Matt. The tennis ball can went flying.

"Look out!" yelled Matt as he dove for the can.

In blink time Milton was out of the cage, leaped to the floor, and dodged under the bed.

"Oh no!" said Kathleen, "I'm sorry. Oh no, Milton got away. Under the bed I think."

Matt started pulling things out from under the bed: his roller blades, his sweatshirt, an old game, baseball glove, old socks, a tennis shoe, and more. "I don't see him anywhere," came his muffled voice. "How can he hide so fast?"

Breathless, Milton panted behind the chest of drawers at the end of the bed. He could not believe he was out of the cage. His inner wild ways were fired up. He was free!

The children looked everywhere. They pulled out every piece of furniture except the chest of drawers, which was too heavy to move. Milton waited, wary, ready to run if they found him. But they didn't.

Finally Matt gave up. "We are back to where we started with that mouse loose in the house," Matt sat on the bed shaking his head. "Mom won't like it. I don't like it either. I want him for a pet. What are we going to do? And anyway what was that all about, Kathleen? Why were you hollering?"

"Oh," she said. "Bertha caught a lizard. I made her let go, and Dad put it in a box. I thought you might want it."

"Well, let's go see," Matt slid off the bed, and together they disappeared down the hallway.

Milton waited till they were gone. He brushed his fur and washed his whiskers to calm down. He peeked around the corner of the chest, spotted a crumpled paper, and pulled it back into his hiding place. He tore up what looked like math homework, made himself a small nest, and crawled into it. He snoozed all day behind the chest of drawers. At bedtime he listened along with Matt to the stereo music. When all was quiet, he crept out from his hiding place, ran across the room and down the hall. Free, he was free!

He dashed to the kitchen and prowled under the table looking for crumbs. He found a few stray morsels, but they were not as tasty as sunflower seeds. He scrambled under the refrigerator and rebuilt his old nest. Water, he needed water. He went looking for Bertha's water dish, but he could not find it. He heard a *swish* from the living room and dashed back under the refrigerator. Bertha rounded the corner, sniffed her way across the room, and prowled right up to the refrigerator. Milton saw her through the grate where he was hiding. He was trapped. He couldn't go anywhere with Bertha around; no running free as long as she stood guard.

The night stretched from minute to minute and into hours. Bertha waited a long time, but finally she tired of the vigil and wandered away for a cat nap. Milton was still thirsty. After a long wait he ventured forth from his hiding place and headed for the living room. He smelled water and sniffed his way to the spot.

He jumped onto the coffee table. Someone had left a paper cup there. *"Water,"* breathed Milton. He crept around the cup looking for a handle to climb on. His tongue was so dry; he needed a drink. He could think of only one way to get it. He stretched up on his hind legs and grasped the lip of the cup with his front paws. He scrabbled with his back feet trying to get  his nose into the cup but instead the cup tipped over. *Splash.* Milton jumped back and *squeaked* as water spilled all over him. It puddled on the table, and some dripped on the carpet.

In a flash Bertha was chasing Milton across the room. He headed for the bookcase by the grand piano and leaped two feet in the air to grab hold of books. Bertha was right behind him, slashing with her paw, and crying, *Mee–owwwww!* Milton squeaked and tumbled onto the piano bench. In one bound he leaped onto the keyboard and scrambled up to the music rack. He dodged behind the rack, saw a hole, and dropped inside the grand piano. He scrambled in the dark, making his way across piano strings, which vibrated with faint tones as his paws slipped over and between the strings. He hopped onto the hammers and sniffed around the felts. They were soft and hard at the same time. He hunkered down beside the hammers and shivered. He was wet.

Mee–owwwww! Bertha prowled around the piano, disgusted. Milton had won again.

Slippers scuffed down the hallway. Kathleen rounded the corner. "Bertha," she scolded in a stage whisper. "Get off that piano bench. Shame on you!" She caught the cat and headed back to her room. "You better sleep in my room, or you are going to get into big trouble. Again." Milton heard the bedroom door shut.

Milton brushed himself all over to dry off. After he was calm, he chewed on one of the felt hammers. It was harder than it looked; he could not get much fuzz off of it. He sneaked back up to the music rack and tore off bits of Matt's music book. He stuffed the paper scraps in his mouth and carried them back to his corner near the hammers where he shaped them into a nest. He went back and forth, back and forth, adding more scraps until the nest was ready. He climbed in and wrapped his tail around him. It was almost morning. He stared across the piano strings. *"So this is where all the music comes from,"* he murmured. Finally, his eyes closed in sleep.

9

Beethoven

"I've got to find that mouse. He's a musical mouse," said Matt. "Milton likes Beethoven."

"How do you know he likes Beethoven?" said Mom, dishing out scrambled eggs.

"He hops around and runs in his wheel when I play the *Contra Dance*." said Matt. "Not only that, when I play the *Moonlight Sonata* on the stereo he comes over and puts his nose against the wire. His ears point toward the sound."

"Amazing," said Mom.

"Maybe you should call him Ludwig," said Kathleen.

Matt ignored Kathleen and helped himself to more toast. "I set him by the piano when I practice, and he seems to like it. Now that gives me an idea. I wonder if he might come back if I set that cage by the piano and left the cage door open. If I played some Beethoven maybe he would crawl back into the cage."

"Well, he might be too far away," said Kathleen. "What about the can? Ludwig always crawls into the can when you are going to clean the cage."

"Don't call him that. There's only one Ludwig," replied Matt. "Maybe I'll put the cage in the bedroom with stereo music," said Matt, "and the can by the piano."

"Two mouse traps. Sounds good," said Dad, setting down his coffee cup.

"I'm going to catch that mouse," said Matt and got up from the table. He hurried down the hallway and into his room. He found the tennis ball can and put in a handful of sawdust and a few seeds. He set the can down beside the bookcase that was next to the piano. In his room, he opened the cage door and checked to be sure there was plenty of water and a granola bar. He pushed things out of the way in front of the cage so Milton could jump up there to get to the open cage door.

Curled up in his piano nest Milton slept until his stomach growled. He turned around in his nest, but it was too early to get up. He stirred again when Matt sat down at the piano and rustled through his music. "Hey, look at this," said Matt. "That mouse chewed a chunk out of the Beethoven *Contra Dance* book. He even ate some notes!"

Milton gulped, *"Notes? Those black things?"* He rubbed his stomach.

"What a mess." Matt straightened his music and gathered up stray bits of paper. He sat down to practice.

Milton bolted upright when Matt began running scales up and down the keyboard. Everything in the piano vibrated. *"I'm buzzing all over,"* muttered Milton. He grabbed onto the closest hammer to steady himself but it abruptly jerked up and down which threw him off balance. He shook himself and began to brush his fur. With great gusto Matt launched into the *Contra Dance*, WAY TOO LOUD! Milton squeaked and tried to get away across the strings. His paws kept falling in between the vibrating strings, which caused a different sound. He slipped and slid to the other side of the harp, but he couldn't get away from the LOUDNESS.

Matt jumped up from the piano bench. "What is going on? This piano sounds crazy. It's really off." He raised the big lid of the piano with both hands and looked inside. "Milton!" he yelled. "That mouse is in the piano. Get out of there. No, wait, where's the can?" He hastily put down the big lid. Milton ran around the harp to the narrow end of the big sounding board and hovered there, quivering.

Matt lifted the lid again and reached for the can he had set on the music rack. Milton didn't waste a moment, with his front paws he grabbed the edge of the piano frame, leaped over the side, and sailed out into space. He held his breath until *flump,* he landed on the carpet and rolled into a ball. He scrambled up and ran, tail flying, feet a–blur. Matt dropped the can and struggled a moment with the heavy lid till he got it down. By that time Milton had crawled into a hole in the back of the stereo set and wiggled past the tangle of wires to a dark corner.

Matt shook his head. "That mouse," he said, "is something else, but I am going to catch him." He picked up the can and fixed it again with sawdust and seeds. He set it back down at the base of the bookcase.

"I will play Milton's favorite piece," said Matt.

"Which one is that?" asked Kathleen.

"The one he ate," glowered Matt, and he launched into the first *Contra Dance.*

Milton slept soundly all day. He woke to a quiet house. His stomach growled, and he was thirsty. He ventured forth from the stereo box and headed for the kitchen. He scooted under the table and found a nibble or two but nothing to fill his empty stomach. No cat around, that was good. He headed for Bertha's water dish, but this time it was empty.

He pricked up his ears when a door *creaked* down the hallway. He started running before he heard the *swish* and then a loud *Mee-owwwww!* Without losing a step Milton veered into the living room sprinting at full speed. Bertha was right on his tail. No time to run for the stereo cabinet, too far to the sofa, Milton spotted the tennis ball can. He sped across the last bit of open carpet and plunged headlong into the can. Bertha pounced at the opening, but she was too late. Milton crouched inside, panting. He saw Bertha's paw stretch toward him but she couldn't quite touch him. She tried the other paw, but again Milton was just out of reach. Disgusted,

Bertha sniffed all around the can. She pushed it with her paw and then her nose. The can rolled on the carpet. Bertha kept pawing and pushing the can across the floor. Milton got a little dizzy trying to stay upright in the rolling can. Sawdust spilled all over him. He shook himself and sneezed. Then *klunk*, the can bumped against the foot pedals of the piano. Bertha kept pawing and bumping the can against the pedals—*klunk . . . klunk . . . klunk.*

Matt stumbled into the living room. "What's going on in here? Bertha, stop that! You woke me up. What have you got there?" Matt hoisted the can into the air and looked inside. "A mouse? I can't believe it! It's Milton! Hurray!" Matt stooped down and petted the cat with his other hand. "Good kitty, good kitty. You caught him for us."

"*Me-oww*," purred Bertha, rubbing against Matt's pajama leg.

Kathleen's slippers scuffed into the room. "Bertha? What are you doing in here? What's happened?"

"Bertha caught the mouse," said Matt. "Look inside. Here he is."

"Saved," said Kathleen.

"*Saved again*," chittered Milton, brushing himself off. He tried to hunker down in the sawdust, but everything moved as Matt carried the can into his bedroom. He slid Milton into the cage, sawdust, seeds and all; then fastened the door shut.

"Here you are," said Matt, "back in your new home. You have food, water, a flower pot to hide in, and a wheel for running. I'll take care of you. You are safe. Here, I'll put on some music for you." Matt pushed the button on the stereo, and the music began.

Milton didn't blink. He popped right into his flower pot home and started pushing sawdust into a nest. He stowed away the seeds and took a drink of water. He was tuckered out. Even though it was nighttime he climbed into his nest and wrapped his tail around him. "*The wild life*," he chittered, "*is for the younger crowd.*"

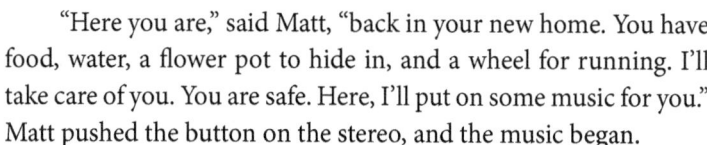

10

Epilogue: The Recital

"WHAT ARE YOU DOING?" asked Kathleen as Matt pounded on a nail. He was kneeling by the fireplace holding a hammer in one hand and a nail in the other. The lid of the tennis ball can lay on a flat piece of firewood.

"I'm pounding holes in the can lid. The metal is tough, but the nail's going through," answered Matt.

"What for?" asked Kathleen.

"For breathing holes," said Matt, "so Milton can stay in the can longer."

"Why?" asked Kathleen, stooping over to watch.

"Well, it's a crazy idea, but I want to take him to my recital. I would like him to hear the Beethoven."

"What was that?" asked Mom, coming into the room.

"My recital," said Matt. "Can Milton come too? He'll be safe in this can, and it's easy to carry along in a bag or something."

"I have a big bag," said Mom.

"I can hold him while you are playing," said Kathleen. "Please, Mom?"

"Hmm," said Mom. "Let me think about it."

"What's that in your hand, Kathleen?" asked Matt, setting down the hammer.

"The song I wrote about Milton," said Kathleen. "Here, want to see it?"

"So you *are* a composer," said Matt, reaching for the manuscript.

"Well, probably not a real composer, just a song writer," said Kathleen.

Mom said, "Any kind of composer is a real one. What's it like? Matt, can you play it?"

Matt sat down at the piano and set the sheet of music against the music rack.

Kathleen leaned over to hold it for him. "I'll sing along," she said, and so they began.

Mom stood behind them and hummed the tune. "Very nice," she said, "a wonderful song. It makes up my mind. I think any mouse who has a song written about him should go to Matt's recital. I think the can idea will work. I think it will be all right, but we have to be really careful and not spill him out. Can you tape the lid shut? It might be better not to tell anyone he is with us. Some people don't like mice."

So Milton went to the recital. Kathleen held the can in her lap, and Milton heard Matt play the Beethoven. The *Contra Dance* tickled his fantastic toes, and he couldn't hold still. Kathleen thought she heard a little tapping from inside the can.

The first movement of the *Moonlight Sonata* warmed Milton's stomach and filled up the empty place inside. When the applause was too loud Milton covered his ears. Afterwards he bumped along inside the can as Matt and Kathleen headed to the car with the family.

"Were you scared, Matt?" asked Kathleen.

"Not really. I just played for Milton like I do at home in the living room," answered Matt. "I knew he was listening."

"Beautiful," said Mom, "it was simply beautiful."

Driving home, Dad quoted: "'. . . And joy shall overtake us as a flood.' That's what Beethoven feels like when you play, Matt. A flood of joy."

"Thanks, Dad." said Matt, who was very pleased.

Epilogue: The Recital

Milton remembered when the creek flooded over the banks. *"Lots of water,"* he chittered to himself. *"Lots of joy."* He couldn't wait to get home.

Back in his cage Milton could not hold still. His stomach was warm and happy. A grand feeling welled up inside him, and he leaped past his wheel onto the side of the cage and scrambled upward. He ran a big loop inside the cage, up one side, upside-down across the top, down the other side, and back; up-across-down-and-back, up-across-down-and-back. Finally he jumped for joy into his wheel and made it *whirrrr*.

Milton didn't settle down until Matt turned on the stereo. The mouse sat with his nose to the cage wire, his ears pointed toward the music. After the Beethoven clicked off, a great silence blanketed the house. Matt lay in his bed unable to sleep. In the stillness he heard a tiny sound coming from Milton's cage. Matt silently rolled over to hear better. It was barely a whisper, but there it was— a faint, musical, mouse trill.

Appendix
Fun Facts

FUN FACTS ABOUT WHITE-FOOTED DEER MICE

1. Deer mice have white feet and a white belly, otherwise their fur ranges from a pale grayish buff color to deep reddish brown depending on where they live.

2. There are numerous species of deer mice. They are abundant and well known in dry-land habitat from Central America north across the United States and into Canada.

3. Tracks made by deer mice are usually a four-print pattern in snow or mud.

4. Deer mice are seedeaters, including nuts. They will open fruit, such as wild cherry, to get to the pit.

5. In the wild deer mice may store as much as a quart of seeds for winter use "in any convenient hole or hollow or cranny."[1]

6. Deer mice are highly adaptable and can find a home almost anywhere.

7. Deer mice make nests in burrows, logs, holes in trees, buildings, bushes, stumps, holes in plowed furrows, among rocks, and on ocean beaches. They have been known to roof over an abandoned bird nest and live in it.

1. *A Field Guide to Animal Tracks* by Olaus J. Murie, Houghton Mifflin (Boston: 1954), p.202.

8. Deer mice nests vary in size from a few inches to nearly a foot in diameter.

9. All mice squeak.

10. Some mice sing. High pitches may not be audible, but lower pitches have been heard. The song is described as a "birdlike trill that can be heard only at a distance of a few feet." Also reported are "little vocal sounds, a rapid series, almost like a chatter, but very faint."

11. Deer mice may seem harmless and innocent, but they can make a mess of stored food and clothing.

12. The life span of deer mice can be up to five and a half years, but few get that old in the wild.

FUN FACTS ABOUT MATT'S FAVORITE COMPOSER, LUDWIG VAN BEETHOVEN

1. Ludwig van Beethoven is considered one of the greatest music composers of all time.

2. He was born in Bonn, Germany, in 1770. He died in Vienna in 1827, at age 56. His grandfather and his father were both musicians.

3. He started piano lessons at four years old. His father was not a good teacher or father, but Beethoven had a lot of talent for music.

4. He later studied with Christian Neefe who was kind to him. Neefe taught Beethoven piano, organ, and composition. Beethoven learned to conduct the court orchestra and to play the violin.

5. He went to Vienna to study with Haydn, one of the city's most famous composers. He learned all about classical music and began composing. He gave concerts to make money.

6. Beethoven had a forceful personality and faced a great many problems. Nevertheless, he made many friends, fell in love,

but never married. He took care of his family. He liked to walk in the countryside, and sometimes scenes from nature can be heard in his music.

7. He composed his most beautiful and extraordinary music while deaf. He was never able to hear some of his greatest music except in his head.

8. Beethoven kept a conversation book at hand so that his friends could write down what they wanted to tell him. The books contain discussions about music and other matters. They give insights into Beethoven's thinking and how to play his music.

9. When he died 20,000 people gathered for his funeral procession and service.

10. The third largest crater on Mercury is named in his honor, as is the main-belt asteroid *1815 Beethoven*. His music is also on the Voyager Golden Record that was sent into outer space with the two Voyager probes.

FUN FACTS ABOUT DAD'S FAVORITE POET, JOHN MILTON, ENGLISH POET AND ESSAYIST

1. John Milton was born in London in 1608 to John and Sara Milton.

2. He was a good student and became interested in poetry very early in life. He loved music, which influenced his poetry. He traveled, read extensively, and in his lifetime learned six languages: Latin, Greek, Italian, Hebrew, French, and Spanish.

3. He is regarded as one of the pre-eminent writers in the English language. His poetry and prose reflect deep personal convictions, a passion for freedom and self-determination, and the urgent issues and political turbulence of his day.

4. He invented new words, usually coined from Latin. He was the first British poet to use non-rhymed verse outside of

the theater. He invented new models and patterns for the rhythms of English verse.

5. While growing up he wrote thoughts and ideas in a "commonplace book" (like a scrapbook). The book is now in the British Library.

6. He was blind by 1660. He wrote most of his major works of poetry after becoming blind. He dictated poems to helpers. Altogether he wrote 1645 poems.

7. John Milton overcame his blindness, a major disability, to write his famous work, *Paradise Lost*. It is thought to be the greatest epic poem in the English language. It is written in blank verse and unrhymed. After *Paradise Lost* was published, the first run of about 1300 copies sold out in eighteen months.

Song: Milton the Mouse

Janice E. Kirk
Words adapted from John Milton

Scamper along

1. A lit - tle mouse named Mil - ton would run and jump and hop____
2. Four paws to go tip - tap-ping A tail to cush-ion slides____
3. Oh when the mer - ry bells ring round And the jo-cund re-becks sound

And when he caught the rhy-thm His feet would nev - er stop____
Oh sport that wrink-led care de -rides And laugh-ter hold-ing both his sides
To many a youth and many a maid Danc - ing in the chec-quered shade

Chorus

Oh seeds and nuts, nuts and seeds, Gra - no - la bars and des - ert weeds,

Come trip it as you go____ On the light fan - tas - tic toe - ho - ho!

Pause for paws

Tip tap your paws

Other Books by Janice E. Kirk

The Christmas Redwood: A Forest Parable
(Wipf & Stock, 2007)

The Road to Beaver Park: Painting, Perception, and Pilgrimage
(Resource Publications, 2016)